MERCER MAYER'S
LC + THE CRITTER KIDS®

THE SWAMP THING

A Golden Book • New York

Western Publishing Company, Inc., Racine, Wisconsin 53404

A Mercer Mayer Ltd./J. R. Sansevere Book

Library of Congress Catalog Card Number: 93-73742
ISBN: 0-307-16660-0/ISBN: 0-307-66660-3 (lib. bdg.)   A MCMXCV

Written by Erica Farber/J. R. Sansevere

Mr. Hogwash and the Critter Kids were going on a class trip to Snake Hill Swamp Sanctuary. They were going to learn all about life in a swamp.

WOLF SPIDERS usually do not spin webs. Instead, they hunt for their prey. They live 1–2 years and have 8 dark eyes, 2 of which are on top of their heads (not pictured).

After school LC went home to pack for his trip. Little Sister gave him her spear shooter—just in case the Swamp Thing came to get him . . .

BINOCULARS are like 2 telescopes put side by side. You can see farther with a telescope, but with binoculars you can see more clearly because you can use both eyes.

The next morning the Critter Kids left for Snake Hill Swamp. After driving for a long time, they finally entered the wetlands.

FOSSILS are impressions or pieces of plants or animals from long ago that died and got buried in mud, sand, or shells. Over time the impressions turned into rock.

When they got to Snake Hill Swamp Sanctuary, the Critter Kids followed Mr. Hogwash to the visitors' center to meet Mrs. Pringle, their guide. She told them that the sanctuary was dedicated to preserving wildlife in their natural habitats.

Mrs. Pringle, Mr. Hogwash, and the Critter Kids all walked out to the start of the boardwalk. Mrs. Pringle's son Roger showed them his pet snake.

GREEN ANOLES can quickly change from green to brown, which makes them hard to find. If you catch one by the tail, don't think you've got it—it'll just drop off its tail and go. Don't worry . . . a new tail will grow.

CAN YOU DO MY BACK?

LIZARDS EAT BUGS FOR FOOD. IF THEY DIDN'T, BUGS WOULD TAKE OVER THE WORLD.

HOW 'BOUT SOME BUG SLIME FOR YOUR BACK?

SAVE THE BUG . . . THAT LIZARD'S ABOUT TO GET IT!

IT'S THE CYCLE OF NATURE.

Everybody walked far out on the boardwalk until they were completely surrounded by trees, plants, and creatures. LC and the Critter Kids were all looking around except for Su Su—she just wanted to sunbathe.

LUBBER GRASSHOPPERS are slow and can't fly. But if you do catch one, hold your nose. When handled, lubbers give off a foul smell. Their spiny back legs can also cut your skin.

SOME OF THE FINEST BIRDS LIVE HERE.

YUCK! GET IT AWAY FROM ME!

OH, REALLY?

HELLO, DOWN THERE.

ISN'T THAT A PRETTY BIRD?

Only female MOSQUITOES will bite you, because they need blood to lay their eggs. They are attracted by the warmth and moisture of your skin.

LC spotted something strange through his binoculars. Roger told him that it could be the Swamp Thing. LC leaned over the rail to get a better look when suddenly he fell right into the water!

Put a DROP OF POND WATER under a microscope and you will see algae and lots of tiny animals.

That night the Critter Kids roasted marshmallows around the campfire. And Roger told them about the Swamp Thing that lived at Snake Hill Swamp.

The SOUTHERN BULLFROG is also called the Pig Frog because of the way its croak sounds. It uses its sticky forked tongue to catch insects and worms.

The Critter Kids went back to their cabins to get ready for bed. Suddenly they heard the strangest sounds. There was something outside their windows! Everybody thought it was the Swamp Thing, but it was just a bunch of frogs.

GREEN TREE FROGS can change color from green to gray. They have toe pads that grip like suction cups, and can attach themselves to plants or even windows.

The next morning Mrs. Pringle took the Critter Kids on a canoe ride. They were looking for her favorite bird—the wood stork.

WOOD STORKS have a 5-foot wingspan, and they eat a lot! A family of 2 adults and 2 young wood storks may eat over 400 pounds of fish in 2 months.

WHOA!

FL 9751

LET'S MOVE ON TO THE MANATEES. THEY LIVE IN THE WATER.

YOU'RE RIGHT, MRS. PRINGLE. WOOD STORKS ARE VERY INTERESTING BIRDS.

Everybody canoed into a bay to see the manatees. Mrs. Pringle told them that manatees are endangered—one of their biggest threats is motorboats that run over them by accident.

After dinner the Critter Kids sat on the porch and watched the sunset. Roger dared them to go to the swamp late that night to see the Swamp Thing . . .

At the stroke of midnight, the Critter Kids followed Roger into the swamp. LC knew there was no such thing as the Swamp Thing. But he couldn't help thinking that if there was, it would definitely live in Snake Hill Swamp.

When you see LIGHTNING, if you count until you hear thunder, you will know how many miles away the lightning is (5 seconds = 1 mile).

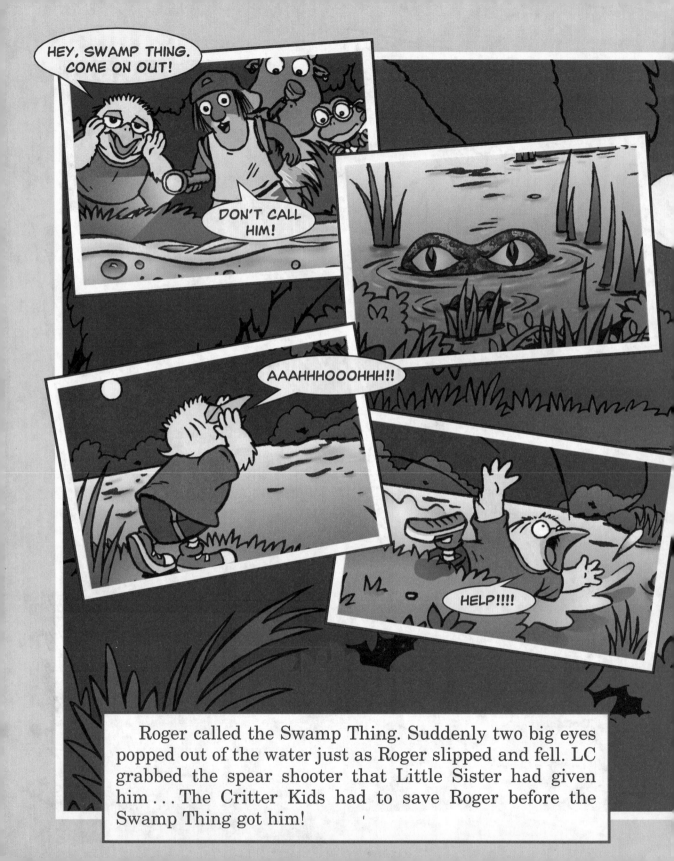

Roger called the Swamp Thing. Suddenly two big eyes popped out of the water just as Roger slipped and fell. LC grabbed the spear shooter that Little Sister had given him ... The Critter Kids had to save Roger before the Swamp Thing got him!

The next day the Critter Kids went home. Mr. Hogwash gave LC a bag full of green chips—he had won the prize! All he had to do was go to Critter Comics and pick it up from Mr. Marvel.

CROCODILES are descendants of a large and ancient group of reptiles that existed in the time of dinosaurs.